PAINKILLER

Titles in Teen Reads:

Badger Publishing Limited, Oldmedow Road, Hardwick Industrial Estate, King's Lynn PE30 4JJ
Telephone: 01438 791037

www.badgerlearning.co.uk

PAINKILLER

TIM COLLINS

Painkiller ISBN 978-1-78464-617-2

Text © Tim Collins 2016
Complete work © Badger Publishing Limited 2016

Publisher: Susan Ross
Senior Editor: Danny Pearson
Editorial Coordinator: Claire Morgan
Copyeditor: Cambridge Publishing Management
Designer: Bigtop Design Ltd
Cover: © Pavel Talashov / Alamy Stock Photo

2 4 6 8 10 9 7 5 3 1

CHAPTER 1

ELEVEN MILES AWAY

Pain shot up my back as I ran past the abandoned cars. I was desperate for Esme to take the hurt away, but I couldn't ask her out here. I needed to wait until we were somewhere more private.

Someone once told me you can still see the dead bodies inside the old cars, forty years after they all got stuck. I never look in the windows just in case it's true.

The last streaks of blue were fading from the sky. We needed to find shelter before it got dark.

I could see a large letter 'M' on top of a long pole ahead of us. I'd seen a few of those before. They were the symbol of an old restaurant called 'McDonald's' that was popular before the great virus.

"Let's try that, Abbie," said Esme. "It could be a hostel."

She raced up the slip road and I hobbled after her. The pain in my back was making me dizzy. We'd gone too far for one day. We should have stopped in the shed a few miles back, but we needed food, and we had to reach a hostel for that.

There were three buildings underneath the large plastic 'M'. One had a long roof, and this used to be a 'petrol station'. Cars would stop there and fill with fuel so they could keep going. The square one would have been a shop, selling crisps and chocolate and magazines. The one on the right with the red roof would have been the McDonald's. Cars used to drive around and collect hot food from the window. Thinking about hot food made my stomach hurt almost as much as my back.

The car park outside the McDonald's was covered with ripped pillows and sleeping bags. A sure sign it was now a hostel.

I felt myself relax. We could buy some berries, maybe even some rat, find a quiet corner and settle down. Then, when no one was looking, Esme could take my pain away by putting her hands on my forehead.

Esme came to a sudden stop and I almost bumped into her. She was gazing at something to the right of the old McDonald's building.

A motorbike. Not a rusty, broken one, like the sort you sometimes saw in the road, but one with a full frame and both wheels. The only people who still had working motorbikes were bounty hunters.

Without saying a word, we turned and ran back to the road.

Bounty hunters are desperate to find painkillers like Esme so they can sell them to the rich. For the past two weeks I'd been trying to get Esme to the commune without any of them finding her.

Back on the road, we weaved around the ancient traffic in the fading light.

I imagined the grinning faces of skeletons rising up inside the cars. I told myself to grow up. I didn't need to worry about dead bodies. I needed to worry about bounty hunters. If one of them got hold of Esme she'd end up imprisoned in the house of a rich person, forced to sooth their pain for the rest of her life.

The throbbing in my back was making my eyes water. Esme hadn't used her powers on me since early that morning and it was getting unbearable.

There was a bridge ahead. We could stop underneath for Esme to take my pain away. It was a huge risk with a bounty hunter so close, but I couldn't go on in such agony, and Esme would never find the commune on her own. Without my help, she'd be captured and imprisoned within hours.

The cars were tightly jammed as we approached the tunnel. Forty years ago they'd all tried to overtake each other in a mad panic and they'd been frozen there ever since.

The great virus had been created by scientists, to help us fight wars. But they hadn't meant it to spread like it did. It had got out of control, sweeping through the world and killing nine out of ten people almost instantly.

I glanced over my shoulder. There was no sign of the bounty hunter or his bike. We could do it if we were quick.

I squeezed through the narrow gap between a faded red car and the cracked concrete of the tunnel. There was a jagged space a few feet down where a van had tried to change lanes. Esme could treat me there.

"I need you to take away my pain," I said. "I can't go on if you don't."

Esme nodded. She never complained when I asked her to treat me. She'd be such a valuable prize for bounty hunters. I couldn't bear the idea of her belonging to one of the rich.

I collapsed into the gap. Esme stepped into the space after me and held out her arms.

We'd done this a thousand times. I knelt on the floor, straightened my back and looked up. Esme stood over me, placed her hands on my temples and closed her eyes.

The pain in my spine disappeared. One moment there was an unbearable thudding, the next there was nothing. If I had a headache, a stomach ache or even just an itch, they'd go too. For a few hours I'd be totally free of discomfort.

Before the great virus, they had places called hospitals where they gave you things called drugs to take your pain away. Now all we have is people like Esme.

I heard a low shuffling from the other side of the tunnel, then a cough, then a muttering voice.

Someone was coming. I could see the dark form of a man clambering over a car towards us.

"I saw that!" he shouted. "You're a painkiller."

CHAPTER 2

TEN MILES AWAY

I stopped and looked back to the tunnel. We'd lost the man after just a few minutes of running.

He hadn't been a bounty hunter, just another ill old man who wanted his pain treating. His neck and forehead had been covered in sores, most of his teeth had gone, he'd been limping and his back had been bent. I was amazed he'd managed to come after us at all.

Maybe he'd drag himself back to his shelter under the bridge now, or maybe chasing us would be the last thing he ever did.

I kept this thought to myself. Esme hates seeing people suffer and leaving the man behind would be on her mind all night. But we had to get to the commune as fast as we could. Stopping for anyone would be too dangerous.

It was almost pitch black now. Thick clouds covered the moon and I had to keep my eyes down to avoid tripping over broken wing mirrors and exhaust pipes.

That's why I didn't spot the hostel until we were almost there.

There was a building called 'Harvester' on our left. It had been a restaurant too, I think. But now it was another hostel, with the usual piles of pillows and sheets outside.

There were no motorbikes around this one. We'd be safe, at least for a while.

Tiredness hit me as soon as I knew rest was coming, and the few metres to the hostel were as hard as the last mile.

Finally we reached a door that had once been glass, but was now boarded with soggy planks of wood.

I held it open for Esme and followed her in. As far as hostels went, it felt pretty safe. The old restaurant tables had been turned on their sides to mark out sleeping areas. Each was filled with dirty sheets, pillows and blankets.

A faded menu was still fixed to the wall next to the door. I couldn't stop myself looking at the old pictures of grilled meat and fries and salad. What must it have been like to point to those meals and have them brought to your table?

A lady in a dusty black coat was sitting on a chair next to the door. I fished some coins out of my pocket. She examined them, nodded and pointed to the far left corner.

We trekked around the maze of tables. On the way, we passed a man in a woollen hat selling old crisp packets filled with berries. I gave him two coins and he handed me two bags.

We settled down in our space in the far corner and ate our berries by the light of a flickering candle. They weren't very ripe, but anything tastes good after a day without food.

I lay down on the pile of yellow sheets next to the wall and felt myself drifting off. Esme took the spot alongside me and I watched her arrange her bedding. Then I closed my eyes and was gone.

It was still dark when I opened them again. But I knew it was almost morning from the pain in my spine. My back problem is the nearest thing I have to a clock.

The space where Esme had been lying was empty.

At first I thought the bounty hunters had taken her. But then I heard her voice from the other side of the hostel.

"It's OK," she was saying. "I can make it better."

I threw the dirty sheets aside and leapt to my feet.

"Stop!" I hissed.

An old lady was kneeling in front of Esme. She was cradling her wrist and blinking tears out of her eyes.

"Thank you," she said. "That's so much better."

A man with a beard in the next area along was sitting up and staring. "What are you two doing?" he asked.

I tried to hurry round the tables to get to Esme, but I was sleepy and slow. I bumped my shin on one of the corners and had to stop and rub it.

"Thank you so much," said the old lady again.

Esme turned to me and I scowled.

"We need to go," I said. "It won't be safe for us now."

People were stirring all around the hostel. A young girl was peering over a table in the middle of the room and rubbing her eyes. A man with a walking stick was forcing himself upright. Even the woman with the dusty coat was looking round from her chair by the door.

The man with the woollen hat was on his feet. He pointed at Esme and shouted, "She's a painkiller. We've got a painkiller here."

CHAPTER 3

NINE MILES AWAY

The sky was already turning pink as we strode along the overgrown strip of grass at the side of the road. We needed to get away fast. As soon as word got out that a painkiller had been spotted, we'd have a hundred bounty hunters after us.

"Why did you do it?" I asked.

"The lady was upset," said Esme. "I could hear crying so I had to find out where it was coming from. Taking her pain away was so simple."

She was always like this. I'd told her over and over again not to treat anyone, but she couldn't stop herself. Since we'd left our compound in the old prison, she'd helped a man with a broken nose, a woman with a twisted ankle and a young boy with bruises up the right side of his face.

"It might have been simple," I said. "But it's made things much more complicated for us. Everyone will come looking for us now."

"I'm sorry," said Esme. "She seemed so upset."

There was a large sign ahead of us. It showed a white circle on a background that would once have been dark green, but was now almost yellow. There were lines coming off the circle with letters and numbers next to them.

I reached into my back pocket and pulled out Jared's scrap of paper. He was the man who'd told us about the commune for painkillers. He'd drawn diagrams of all the signs we'd see along the way and marked out the route we had to take.

I scanned down the paper to find a drawing that matched the sign. It was there, near the bottom. A circle with arrows marking out roads called A332, A303, M4 and M25. We had to take the third one, the M4.

"Are we near the commune yet?" asked Esme.

Jared had drawn about thirty diagrams and there were only six left. According to his notes, we just had to stay on the M4 for nine miles and we'd be there.

"Almost," I said.

The road ahead opened into a large roundabout. Jared had told me about these things. They meant cars could change onto other roads more quickly.

I wondered why saving time had been so important. But it's hard to understand why anyone acted how they did back then. Things were so different.

When the great virus struck in 2024, it killed nearly everyone. A small group of people weren't affected by it, but no one ever found out why. Most of the scientists were dead, and the ones left were too busy trying to survive like everyone else.

To imagine what things were like in the old times, you had to start with large crowds everywhere. Every shop, every road and every park was as packed as a hostel on a winter night.

When you'd got your head around that, you could start to imagine all the speeding cars, all the small glowing rectangles of glass, all the different types of hot food, and all the giant metal planes in the sky.

Whenever I tried to picture those days it made my head swim.

We were at the roundabout now. This place must have been chaos when the great virus struck. A huge truck was on its side, covering three lanes.

Its frame had twisted and its back doors had fallen off to reveal the dark crooked space within.

Three cars had slammed into it. Their frames had crumpled against the bottom of the vehicle and other cars had gone into the back of those. A big crash like that was called a 'pile-up'.

The only way past was to climb over the bonnets and hope they weren't so rusty that our feet went right through.

I'd just pushed myself onto the first one when I heard something.

The distant spluttering of a motorbike engine. A bounty hunter was coming.

Esme was staring back down the road and chewing her little finger.

"Someone from the hostel must have tipped them off," I said.

"I'm sorry," she said. "I just wanted to take the old lady's pain away."

"It doesn't matter now," I said. "We need to get out of sight."

The engine was getting louder. We wouldn't have more than a couple of minutes before the bounty hunter was here.

We needed to get off the road, but I couldn't work out where to go. The land was flat to every side and there were no obvious hiding places. There was a field to our right with wild, overgrown grass. Maybe we could duck down and crawl through it. But we'd make a path anyone could spot.

To our left was a wet field with a thick hedgerow at the far end. We could hide behind that if we could make it in time. But it was too far away. We wouldn't even get halfway there.

Maybe the best thing would just be to keep going down the M4 as we'd planned. If we crawled along the ground we wouldn't be spotted from the roundabout. Then we'd just have to hope the bounty hunter chose one of the other two roads instead.

Esme tapped the side of truck.

"In here," she said. "Quick."

I climbed back down from the bonnet. I wasn't sure about Esme's plan, but I didn't have a better one.

"He's bound to see us in there," I said.

"Not if we go right to the back and press ourselves against the side," said Esme. "It's twisted round, so you can't see all the way in. He'd have to get off his bike and step inside."

It was too late to come up with an alternative. We'd have to go with it.

We ran inside the overturned truck. The bottom was covered in a thin pool of stagnant water. Our footsteps echoed as we splashed through. There were dark shapes bobbing about that were probably rats. I hoped they were dead.

When we got to the back, we pushed ourselves into the frame. A huge dent now shielded us from the road.

I felt rotten water seeping in through the holes in my shoes as the bike got nearer. We needed to stay perfectly still, and pray the bounty hunter didn't look in.

CHAPTER 4

EIGHT MILES AWAY

I peered over the top of the hedge. The bounty hunter had stepped off his bike and was looking around. I ducked down to the muddy ground.

Esme's plan had worked. The bounty hunter had driven past the twisted truck. He'd gone straight ahead at first, letting us make our way down the M4 for about a mile. But he'd soon realised he'd gone the wrong way. We'd heard him coming back, dashed across the field on our right and scrambled through a gap in the hedgerow.

"He'll spot our tracks soon," said Esme. "He'll know we came this way."

"We can keep going across the fields," I said. "He'll never be able to follow on his bike and he won't risk abandoning it, no matter how much he thinks you're worth."

I looked across the field we'd found ourselves in. It was marked by another thick hedge to our left and a high wire fence in the distance. There was a strip of dry grass running along the hedge, but otherwise everything was a deep bog. This whole area still hadn't recovered from the big floods three months ago.

I pointed at the wire fence. "Let's try and make it over that. Then we can follow the direction of the M4 from a safe distance."

We crept alongside the hedge, stooping low to stay out of sight.

This was going to slow us down. On the road, we could have reached the commune by the evening. Over these muddy fields, we'd have to keep going through the night.

We wouldn't be able to stop in a hostel and we couldn't get any food. There were berries on the hedge that looked like the ones the man in the woollen hat had sold us. But I couldn't be sure they were the same kind. They could be poisonous for all I knew.

I told myself to focus on the journey and stop thinking about food.

"If this is getting too difficult I can give myself up," said Esme. "I don't mind working for whoever the bounty hunter sells me to. I'll make sure you can come too, so I can still treat your back."

"It wouldn't work," I said. "The bounty hunters would never let me stay with you. They'd kill me for trying to hide you. And you would mind working for the rich when you met them. Those people got where they are through violence and cheating. You'd end up as a miserable slave, kept alive only for your powers."

I looked behind and saw Esme's hand trembling as she brushed away an overhanging clump of hedge. It was so hard to explain how serious things were without upsetting her.

"But it will never come to that," I said. "We'll be at the commune soon and you'll be with others just like you. The bounty hunters can't get you there."

Every time I explained this to Esme I felt my heart sink. I'm not a painkiller, so I wouldn't be allowed to join the commune too. I'd have to return to our old compound in the prison and live with my bad back for the rest of my life.

The ache was returning now, as if to remind me what I had to look forward to. It was just a small throb in the base of my spine, but soon it would spread up to my shoulders and make me hunch forward.

It didn't matter. My job was to get Esme to the commune, not to worry about myself. Everyone has to live with their pain now. That's just how the world is.

Ever since Jared had told us about the commune I knew I'd have to take Esme there. She was too trusting to be safe anywhere else. Even if I got captured by the bounty hunters afterwards it wouldn't matter. I'd have done something worthwhile, and how many people can say that these days?

We reached the tall fence. It was made from wooden stakes struck deep into the ground and connected by a mesh of rusty metal.

I stepped up and gave it a shake. The top swung back and forth but the stakes didn't budge. They were still firmly rooted in the ground, decades after they were planted.

"We can't push it down," I said. "We'll have to climb over."

"You go first," said Esme. She crouched at the bottom of the fence and cupped her hands together. "This will make it easier."

I put my right foot in Esme's hands and she pushed me up. Clinging to the top of the fence, I heaved my feet over. They swung to the other side and struck the metal. I felt a sharp sting in my back and wished I'd got Esme to treat me before testing out my acrobatic skills.

There was a loud crack and the fence started to creak back. I whipped my head to the side and saw the wooden stakes were keeling over in the soft ground. If I'd held on, the fence might have lowered me slowly, but I panicked and tried to climb down.

I lost my grip and plummeted to the field below, crashing onto the small of my back.

Pain shot up my spine and along my arms and legs. I felt my eyes filling with tears and my legs and arms shaking.

It was Esme I thought of as I let out a scream. She'd never make it to the compound now, and it was all my fault.

CHAPTER 5

ONE MILE AWAY

Esme took her hands off my temples and I gazed up at the sky. My pain was gone and I could focus on things again. The sun was rising ahead of us, casting long shadows over the swampy ground.

I was wrong about it taking us a whole night to get across the fields. It had actually taken us two. Since I'd fallen from the fence, I could only go a few hundred metres at a time without collapsing. Esme had needed to use her painkilling powers on me over and over again.

The pain was just as strong every time it returned. Whatever I'd done to my back, it wasn't getting any better. I'd be living with even more discomfort from now on, and soon I wouldn't have Esme to help me.

There was no way I could climb over anything, so we'd taken huge detours to search for gaps in the hedges and fences.

We were back on the motorway now. Esme helped me to my feet and I hobbled along the sloping grass at the side of the road. At least we didn't have to worry about the bounty hunter anymore. He'd never have guessed it would take us two whole days to get down this short stretch of road.

There was another faded green sign ahead. I took Jared's piece of paper out of my pocket and looked for a drawing that matched it.

It was right at the bottom. According to his notes, the commune should be on the slip road a few hundred metres ahead. I broke away from Esme and strode on, ignoring the stiffness in my legs.

There was another sign ahead. It had been washed almost blank by years of rain, but I could still make out some symbols on a pale blue background.

Jared had mentioned this in his notes too. An arrow pointing left, followed by a petrol pump, followed by a fork and spoon crossed over each other, followed by a bed. The first picture meant you could fill your car with petrol, the second meant you could buy some food and the third meant you could rent a room in a hotel.

The hotel had been known as the 'Premier Inn' in the days before the great virus. It was now the painkiller commune.

We were almost at our destination.

I turned around to Esme and stuck my thumbs up. She grinned back.

I found myself jogging down the slip road. I'd barely been able to walk since my fall, but now I was almost running. I'd pay for it next time my back flared up, but I didn't care. We were so close.

The road curved around to the left, cutting through a clump of trees. I dashed around the remains of a head-on collision between a delivery van and a small car.

There it was. A wide building with five floors and the words 'Premier Inn' on the front. It had taken us over two weeks to get here, but we'd finally made it.

I got my breath back while Esme caught up.

'Is that the building with the other painkillers?' asked Esme.

"Yes," I said. "Unless Jared was lying to us."

"What do you think they'll be like?" asked Esme.

I had no idea. No one knew anything about painkillers really. No one knew what gave them their powers. No one knew why so many had been born since the great virus. All anyone knew was that they wanted them around.

"Let's find out," I said.

The sun was rising just above the roof of the Premier Inn. I had to shield my eyes to get a proper look at it. Most of the windows and doors were still intact, which was rare for such a large building. This meant someone had protected it, which was good. But something about it wasn't quite right.

I worked out what it was. There were no barriers to keep people out. Our old compound had once been a prison. It had high brick walls and coils of sharp barbed wire. But this place had nothing to stop people wandering in. There were no guards, no moats, no watchtowers. Just an empty car park and a wide front door.

I was hoping to hear voices inside as we approached, but it was totally silent. There were no dark shapes moving around at the windows and the old curtains weren't twitching. The whole place seemed empty.

I felt my heart sink. This couldn't be true. Not after all the struggles of the last two weeks – trekking over boggy fields, hiding from bounty hunters, ignoring my throbbing back. It couldn't have all been for nothing.

I pushed the front door open, leaving a handprint on the dusty glass.

The building was totally dark. There were no flickering candles on the floor or the curved white desk ahead of us.

"Hello?" I shouted. "Is anyone here?"

There was no reply.

This couldn't be right. Surely there was a secret area where the real commune was. Perhaps we'd find a staircase to a huge underground base, or I'd press a button and one of the walls would flip round.

We continued past the curved desk into a gloomy corridor. The doors on either side were open. Each room contained a tidy desk and a perfectly made bed. They all had sheets, pillows and blankets. I'd never seen anything like them before, except in books and magazines from before the great virus.

This meant the place was being looked after by someone. The beds should have been stripped years ago, like the ones in every other hotel and house. Why would an empty building be in such a good state? After two nights without sleep, my brain was sluggish and I couldn't make sense of it.

My best explanation was that the commune had only been abandoned very recently. If this was right, they were bound to have left a clue about where they'd gone. It would mean our journey hadn't been in vain, but it might also mean we still had a long way to go.

We got to the end of the corridor and peered into another empty room.

Esme wandered in and sat down on the edge of the bed. 'It doesn't matter that the others aren't here,' she said. 'We did our best.'

"I think they were here until just a few days ago," I said. 'I bet they left instructions about where they went.'

I sat down next to Esme. The mattress felt amazingly soft after all the hard ground I'd sat on recently. 'Let's search every room for a note. It could be inside one of the drawers, tucked under a carpet or hidden under a bed.'

But I felt myself flopping backwards as I spoke. After two nights trekking through muddy fields, I wouldn't have been able to resist a dirty pile of rags in the corner of a hostel. This was an actual

bed with a mattress and a pillow. I had
no chance.

My half of the bed raised slightly as Esme lay
down next to me.

I was asleep in seconds.

CHAPTER 6

THREE MILES AWAY

I woke up in total darkness. It couldn't have been noon when we went to bed, so we must have slept for at least nine hours.

From the throbbing in my back, I guessed it had been much longer. I had a feeling it was after midnight.

I really needed Esme to take my pain away, but I decided to let her sleep. I'd lie here biting my fist until morning if it meant she could rest more.

There was loud breathing in the room. At first I thought it was Esme snoring, but I soon realised it was coming from the open doorway.

Someone was standing there and staring at us. I began to make out the outline of a tall figure.

I propped myself up on my elbows, setting off a fresh surge of pain and making myself wince.

"Who are you?" I asked.

Beside me, Esme stirred and stretched her arms out.

"What time is it?" she asked.

"Shh," I said. "There's someone there."

Esme bolted upright. Her breathing sped up as she stared at the doorway.

For a moment there was just Esme's fast panting and the slow breathing in the doorway.

Then a man spoke. "Why have you come here?"

"We were told about this place by someone called Jared who lived in our compound," I said.

"I don't know anyone by that name," said the man.

I fished Jared's scrap of paper out of my pocket and held it up. It was too dark for him to see and I'm not sure what it would have proved anyway. I just felt I needed to give some evidence that we hadn't just wandered in to sleep.

"Are you a bounty hunter?" I asked.

"Why would a bounty hunter be interested in you?" he asked. "Are you a painkiller?"

My back was making it hard to think straight. I didn't want to give too much away, but I didn't have the energy to lie.

"No," said Esme. "But I am."

"Then you should come with me," said the man.

"Why?" I asked. "So you can sell her to some rich guy as a slave?"

"No," said the man. "So I can take her to a commune where people like us can be safe. It's three miles from here. We can be there in an hour."

I heard myself let out a sigh and felt tears well in my eyes. Could it really be true that Esme would reach the commune after all? That everything we'd been through hadn't been in vain?

I tried not to let myself believe it. I had no reason to trust this man yet. He could be taking her straight into the compound of a rich person.

"Jared told us this hotel was the commune," I said. "Why do you need to take her somewhere else?"

"We don't give out the real location to anyone," said the man. "But there are a few entry points we watch over. I keep an eye on this one; other painkillers look after the rest. If I think someone's wandered in just to sleep or steal things, I tell them to leave. If I think someone's looking for the commune, I watch them for a while to work out if they're genuine."

The man stalked round to Esme's side of the bed and pulled one of the curtains aside. Weak moonlight streaked in and I got a clearer glimpse of him. He was wearing a long coat and a hat with a wide brim.

He lifted something out of his pocket.

I gasped. It was a knife.

I tried to pull myself up but the pain in my back made me sink down again.

"Don't worry," he said. "This is for me, not her."

He cut the end of his finger, put the knife back in his pocket and knelt down next to Esme.

"Take the pain away," he said.

Esme glanced at me and I nodded.

She turned back to him and put her hands on his temples.

After a moment of silence, he said, 'OK. I believe you. You're one of us. You can come.'

I forced myself upright again.

"And why should she believe you?" I asked. "You could be a bounty hunter for all we know."

He didn't reply. Instead, he walked over to my side of the bed.

When he was level with me, he thrust his hands forward. I flinched back.

"I'm not going to hurt you," he said. "The exact opposite, in fact."

He reached out again and this time I let him put his hands on my temples.

The pain in my back went instantly. He was a painkiller, maybe an even more powerful one than Esme.

So he'd been telling the truth after all. He was going to take her to the commune. She was safe.

Now the tears came. They poured down my cheeks as I grabbed Esme's hand and squeezed it.

CHAPTER 7

HERE

We've been at the commune for two weeks now. It was an army base before the great virus, and they've managed to keep all the giant fences in place.

It must be one of the safest places in the world.

And yesterday they gave me some very good news. I can stay here too.

When painkillers are accepted into the commune, they're allowed to bring their families. Friends aren't usually allowed, but when the elders interviewed Esme, they agreed to bend the rule. They said we're pretty much family anyway.

We've both been given rooms in Accommodation Block D that are like the ones in the Premier Inn, with proper beds and desks and candles.

The man who brought us here is called Ray. He spends most of his time monitoring the Premier Inn and protecting it from thieves. But if we ever see him around here he's very friendly to us.

Last week he gave us some marker pens to draw on our walls. I used mine to copy out Jared's diagrams so I'll always remember our journey.

My back is aching again now, so I need to go and find Esme. I'm surrounded by genuine painkillers, and any of them would fix it if I asked. But I know how much she enjoys it so I always wait for her.

I hope one day the world will be safe for painkillers like Esme and they'll be able to leave the commune and help people. In the meantime, I'll never forget how lucky I am to have one as my best friend.

THE END

ABOUT THE AUTHOR

Tim Collins is originally from Manchester, but now lives near London. He has written over 50 books, including *Wimpy Superhero*, *Dorkius Maximus*, *Cosmic Colin* and *Monstrous Maud*. His other titles in the Teen Reads series are *Dawn of the Daves*, *Troll*, *The Locals*, *Joke Shop*, *Mr Perfect* and *Wasteland*. He has won awards in the UK and Germany.